The
Littlest
Star

To the staff and volunteers
at Shooting Star Chase,
bringing sparkle to little lives
when it matters most
R.L.

For my Dad
D.K.

Text copyright © 2016 Richard Littledale
Illustrations copyright © 2016 Dubravka Kolanovic
This edition copyright © 2016 Lion Hudson plc/Tim Dowley Associates Ltd

The right of Richard Littledale to be identified as the author and of Dubravka Kolanovic to be identified as the illustrator of this work has been asserted by them in accordance with the Copyright, Designs and Patents Act 1988.

Published by Lion Children's Books
an imprint of
Lion Hudson plc
Wilkinson House, Jordan Hill Road,
Oxford OX2 8DR, England
www.lionhudson.com/lionchildrens

ISBN 978 0 7459 7695 2

First edition 2016

A catalogue record for this book is available from the British Library

Printed and bound in China, July 2016, LH06

The Littlest Star

Richard Littledale

Illustrated by Dubravka Kolanovic

LION
CHILDREN'S

Have you ever wondered how
many stars there are in the
great big sky?

He couldn't shoot as high as some.

He didn't have a long, shiny
tail to tow across the heavens
behind him.

A very clever scientist once worked out that if you counted all the grains of sand on all the beaches in all the countries of the whole wide world, they still wouldn't be as many as the stars in the sky.

And of course, all the stars are the same… or are they?
I want to tell you about the littlest star of all.
He wasn't as bright and sparkly as some of the others.

He couldn't shoot as high as some.

He didn't have a long, shiny
tail to tow across the heavens
behind him.

In fact, he really wasn't terribly exciting at all.
Sometimes, when all the other stars were whirling
and sparkling and dancing in the heavens…

… he would find a
quiet little patch of sky
all to himself.

And that's just where he was when God's angel found him.
    He called to him softly by name – though I won't tell you the name, as the names of the stars are so spectacular they only sound silly when you and I say them.

"God has a special job for you,"
said the angel.

"For me?" said the littlest star, his face lighting up even more than it usually did.

The angel nodded his golden head, and the littlest star swished along behind him to find out what this job might be.

Carefully, in his big, deep voice, God explained that he had a gift to make to the world below.

"My Son is to be born tonight," he said. "He won't have a palace, or even a house, or even a cot to sleep in. Would you shine your best and most golden light on him?"

The littlest star was far too excited to speak, and just bobbed his little head up and down in excitement.

"Off you go, then!" God said.

And with a swish of golden sparks, the littlest star zoomed off… to shine on the place where the baby lay.

For many days he stayed there, beaming down on the stable where baby Jesus was tucked up cosily in the straw.

Shepherds came and went beneath him, and the littlest star looked down at them.

Just when he felt he could not stretch out his little starry arms any longer, he spotted three strangers, away in the distance.
They rode on huffy camels and carried sparkly bags – and he could see just where they were heading.

He took it upon himself to guide them the last little bit of the journey – across the desert… into the town, and down the narrow roads and alleyways.

When their journey was finally over, just before they
ducked into the tiny door of the stable… the three
looked right up at the littlest star, and each bowed
his head in thanks.

The littlest star's special job was done and he swished
back up to the skies to join all the others.

   He doesn't mind now if some stars are bigger,
or shinier, or faster than him, because he knows
what happened so many years ago.

But he's still special, and if you creep
outside and look really, really hard, you
might just find him.

Other Titles from Lion Children's Books

The Christmas Story for Little Angels
Julia Stone & Dubravka Kolanovic

The Extra Special Baby *Antonia Woodward*

My Bible Story Book *Sophie Piper & Dubravka Kolanovic*

Not So Silent Night! *Rebecca Elliott*

Tales from Christmas Wood *Suzy Senior & James Newman Gray*